No Dogs Allowed

Ready, Set, Dogs!

No Dogs Allowed

Ready, Set, Dogs!

WHOOSH!

Stephanie Calmenson & Joanna Cole
illustrated by Heather Ross

SQUARE
FISH

Henry Holt and Company
New York

SQUARE
FISH

An Imprint of Macmillan
175 Fifth Avenue
New York, NY 10010
mackids.com

Library of Congress Cataloging-in-Publication Data
Calmenson, Stephanie.
No dogs allowed / Stephanie Calmenson and Joanna Cole ; illustrations
by Heather Ross.
      pages   cm.—(Ready, set, dogs! ; 1)
Summary: Best friends and dog lovers Kate and Lucie live in apartments
where dogs are not allowed, but a pair of unusual necklaces they find
in a thrift store allow them to become dogs whenever they wish.
ISBN 978-1-250-04414-3 (paperback) • 978-0-8050-9646-0 (e-book)
[1. Dogs—Fiction. 2. Best friends—Fiction. 3. Friendship—Fiction.
4. Shapeshifting—Fiction. 5. Contests—Fiction. 6. Humorous stories.]
I. Cole, Joanna. II. Title.
PZ7.C136Nnm 2013   [Fic]—dc23   2013017884

Originally published in the United States by Henry Holt and Company
First Square Fish Edition: 2014
Book designed by Ashley Halsey
Square Fish logo designed by Filomena Tuosto

1 3 5 7 9 10 8 6 4 2

To Emily, Joshua, Noah, and Justin
—S. C.

To Annabelle and William
—J. C.

Contents

No Dogs Allowed

Ready, Set, Dogs!

The Lucky Find

Early one morning the clock radio went off in Kate Farber's room. Kate popped up in bed. *Wonka-wonk!* Amos-on-the-Airwaves was honking a horn into the microphone.

Is there a car in here? thought Kate.

She looked around her room for cars. Of course there weren't any. It was just Amos finishing his traffic report. Amos Adams was Tuckertown's favorite radio announcer, and everyone loved to listen to him.

Amos had stopped honking and started barking. *Woof-arf-yip!*

Kate looked around her room. It was as neat as a pin, and there were dogs everywhere. They were on her sheets and pajamas. They were dancing across her lamp shade. There were knickknack shelves filled with little glass dogs all lined up in neat rows.

Kate loved dogs. But there would never be a real one in her room. She lived in a garden apartment where the rule was NO DOGS ALLOWED. Kate was a sensible girl. She knew there was no point in begging for a dog. But that didn't stop her from wishing for one.

She was wishing for one when Amos got her attention with the word *contest*.

"It's Adopt-a-Dog Week, and we're having a song-writing contest," he said. "We need a catchy song to get people out adopting dogs from the Tuckertown Shelter. *Woof-arf-yip!* Start writing and send your songs in pronto!"

Pronto means "quickly." That was just right for Kate. Kate did everything quickly.

She quickly grabbed her glasses from her night table and put them on. The brown frames looked good with her freckles and dark-brown hair.

Then she speed-dialed her best friend, Lucie Lopez.

Kate knew what Lucie would be hearing at the other end. She'd be hearing the special ring they had programmed on their phones. *Arfa-arf! Arfa-arf!*

Lucie wished she could have a dog, too. But she lived in the same garden apartment building, right next door to Kate. So, instead of a real dog, she had thirty-two stuffed dogs facing every which way in her room. She also had tons of books about dogs. They were piled up in stacks on her dresser, chairs, and even the floor. She had read every single one more than once.

Lucie's room was as messy as Kate's room was neat.

Kate pressed the speaker button on her phone and started getting dressed while Lucie's phone kept ringing. *Arfa-arf!*

Lucie finally picked up on the fourth *arf*. Lucie definitely was not a morning person.

"Hullo," she said sleepily, pushing her ginger-colored bangs out of her eyes.

"Quick! Meet me outside," said Kate, tying her right sneaker.

"I'm still sleeping," said Lucie.

"No, you're not. You're talking," said Kate, tying her left sneaker. "We've got a song to write, a contest to win! Amos says the dogs at the shelter need our help."

"Huh?" said Lucie.

"I'll explain outside," said Kate. "Hurry up and get dressed. I'm wearing my Dalmatian tee."

"Mine's in the laundry," said Lucie, yawning. "I'll wear my pink poodle shirt. I got new pink ribbons to match."

"Of course you did," said Kate.

Lucie loved ribbons. And she definitely loved pink.

Kate and Lucie had been best friends since they were little. They thought they were the luckiest girls in the world to be living right next door to each other.

By the time they hung up, Lucie had swung her legs out of bed and put one foot on the floor. *Squawk!* She had stepped on an old stuffed dog that had a squeaker in it.

How did that get there? thought Lucie.

Meanwhile, Kate was already dressed and

had tied her hair in pigtails. She grabbed a breakfast bar and headed outside.

On the way, she heard her mom call, "Please take the bag in the hall to the thrift shop!"

"Got it!" said Kate, sweeping up the bag on her way out.

Kate sat on her front steps to wait for Lucie. She didn't like waiting, but with Lucie for a best friend, she was used to it. While she waited, she hummed a tune and tapped her feet. Five minutes later, Lucie came out.

"Another trip to the thrift shop?" Lucie said when she saw the bag at Kate's feet.

"My mom's on a cleaning mission," said Kate, jumping up. "Let's go!"

Kate and Lucie started toward the Lucky Find Thrift Shop. They went there a lot, mostly just to look around. And whenever they bought something, they liked knowing the money went to charity.

"Wait till you hear about the song contest!" said Kate. She told Lucie all about it.

"Maybe we could win and help the dogs!" said Lucie. "We're great at rhyming." Then she added, "We do it all the timing."

Kate rolled her eyes. Lucie ignored her and started singing:

Adopt a puppy!
It's better than a guppy!

"I like it!" said Kate. She took a turn.

Adopt a dog.
It's better than a hog!

As they walked to the thrift shop, the song got sillier and sillier.

"Hi, Mrs. Bingly!" they called as they walked through the door of the Lucky Find.

"Hi, girls," said Mrs. Bingly, the store owner. "What have you got there?"

Kate set the bag on the counter. "Mom's cleaning her closet again," she said.

"Wonderful," said Mrs. Bingly, taking the bag to the back of the store.

"Hey, Kate, look at this!" called Lucie.

Lucie was modeling a hot-pink hat with six kinds of fruit on the brim. It was draped with ribbons. Just right for Lucie.

She noticed a fluffy purple boa and tossed it around her neck.

She got a bright-green pocketbook and hung it on her shoulder.

"How many things are you going to try at once?" said Kate, being her usual sensible self.

"Maybe I'll try on shoes next," said Lucie.

"If you keep going, you'll be wearing everything in the store," said Kate.

Lucie didn't worry about being sensible. A display of sparkly necklaces had already caught her eye.

"Look at the two with the pink dog bones

hanging down," she said, putting all the other stuff back.

Even Kate couldn't be sensible once she saw those necklaces.

"Let's try them on," she said. "They're perfect for Adopt-a-Dog Week."

"They're perfect for us!" said Lucie.

The girls each grabbed a necklace and went into the fitting room so they could look in the mirror.

"Help me with the clasp," said Lucie.

"Got it," said Kate. "Now help with mine."

They turned to admire themselves.

"These look great on us!" said Lucie.

"Let's get them!" said Kate.

"Woofa-woof!" they said together, giving each other high fives.

Woofa-wow! Kate and Lucie had no idea they were about to get the surprise of their lives.

The instant their hands touched, the necklaces lit up and there was a pop and a whoosh in the fitting room of the Lucky Find Thrift Shop.

When the smoke cleared, Lucie and Kate couldn't believe their eyes. Two dogs were staring straight at them from the mirror.

Those Dogs Are Us!

"How did those dogs get in here?" said Kate. She looked behind her. No dogs.

Lucie looked under the fitting room chair. No dogs.

They looked in the mirror again. The two dogs were still there, staring back at them.

Kate and Lucie looked at each other. Out of the corner of their eyes, they could see the dogs looking at each other.

Lucie cocked her head. The dog in the mirror cocked its head.

Kate wiggled her behind. The dog in the mirror wiggled its behind.

"It can't be," said Kate.

"No way," said Lucie.

"Are you thinking what I'm thinking?" asked Kate.

"You mean that those dogs in the mirror are *us*?" said Lucie.

"Exactly," said Kate. "It's ridiculous, isn't it?"

"It's impossible," said Lucie.

They studied the dogs. The one looking at Lucie was shaggy with ginger-colored fur hanging almost to her eyes. The fur looked a lot like Lucie's bangs.

The dog in front of Kate was white with brown ears, tan spots, and patches around her eyes. The ears looked a lot like Kate's pigtails. The spots looked like her freckles. The patches were like her glasses.

Both dogs had silver collars with pink dog

bones twinkling in the light. They were just like the dog-bone necklaces that . . .

"Aaahhhh!" Kate and Lucie screamed together.

"Is everything okay in there, girls?" called Mrs. Bingly.

"Girls?" whispered Kate. "We're not girls anymore. We're dogs!"

"Everything's fine!" called Lucie.

"Fine? What do you mean fine?" hissed Kate. "We just turned into dogs!"

"How do you like the necklaces?" called Mrs. Bingly.

"They're fine, too!" called Lucie.

"Except that now they're dog collars," whispered Kate.

"Why don't you come out and show them to me?" said Mrs. Bingly.

"Oh, great. How are we going to get out of here?" whispered Kate.

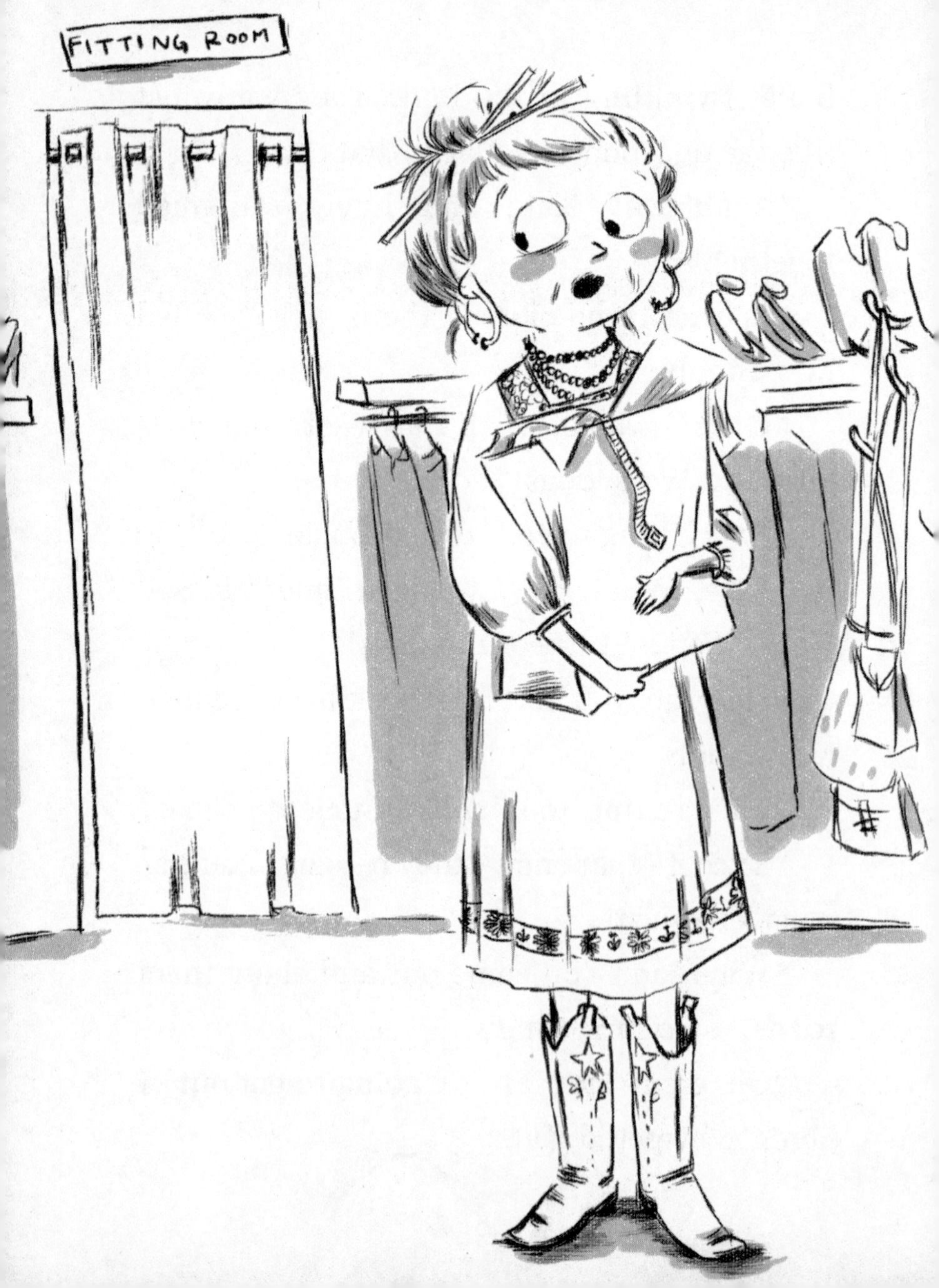
FITTING ROOM

"Follow me," said Lucie.

She got down low and slinked under the curtain of the fitting room.

Mrs. Bingly had started arranging tea sets on a shelf. The dogs crawled past her.

"So far, so good," whispered Lucie.

"Watch out!" whispered Kate.

Oops! Too late. Lucie had bumped into a mannequin dressed in a lacy evening gown. It started toppling over. As Mrs. Bingly grabbed the mannequin, she looked down.

"Dogs? How did dogs get in here?" she shouted.

Kate and Lucie jumped up and started to run. Mrs. Bingly was right behind, shooing them out.

Lucie looked over her shoulder and knocked into a rack of scarves. A blue striped scarf fell on her back. A red striped one draped over her eyes.

Just then the door opened and a customer walked in. With the scarf over her eyes, Lucie couldn't see a thing. She ran right into the man and knocked him down.

Kate used her teeth to pull the scarves off Lucie. Then they jumped over the customer together.

Mrs. Bingly raced to help the man up.

"Out, out!" she yelled at the dogs. "Can't you read?"

"I hope we still *can* read," said Kate as they ran out the door.

When they got outside, they looked back at

the sign in the window. They still *could* read. And the sign was the same as the one at their apartments. In big black letters, it said:

NO DOGS ALLOWED!

Dogs? What Dogs?

"Stop sniffing me!" said Kate.

"I can't help it. Everything smells amazing—even you!" said Lucie.

"Get a whiff of this garbage can," Kate said as they passed Patty's Pizza.

Lucie was there in an instant. She scarfed down an old pizza crust lying on the ground.

"Yuck, you just ate garbage!" said Kate.

"I know. It was delicious," said Lucie.

Then they passed a window and saw their reflections.

Boing! Kate's tail went straight up in the air.

Shimmy, shimmy, shimmy! Lucie wagged her tail so fast, her whole backside went from side to side.

"We really are adorable as dogs," said Kate. "I love your shaggy coat."

"I love your spots," said Lucie.

"I love our dog-bone collars," said Kate.

"Maybe we can get dog sweaters with ribbons," said Lucie.

"Puh-lease!" said Kate, rolling her eyes.

They were trotting along, when suddenly they stopped in their tracks.

Sniff, sniff.

"Do you smell what I smell?" said Lucie.

"You mean Banana-Fandana gum?" said Kate.

Thanks to their new, super-dog noses, the girls could smell it all the way down the street.

DJ Jackson always chewed three pieces of gum at once. He said it gave him the full flavor.

Thunk, thunk, thunk.

"Do you hear what I hear?" said Kate.

"You mean Danny's basketball?" said Lucie.

Danny DeMarco always bounced his basketball while he walked. If he wasn't bouncing it, he was spinning it on his finger. If he wasn't spinning it, he was taking jump shots.

Sure enough, DJ and Danny turned the corner. They were the two most annoying boys on the planet.

With their super-dog ears, the girls could hear every word

the boys were saying, even though they were still far away.

"I bet Lucie and Kate are going to enter Amos's song contest," said Danny. "Whatever they come up with will be goofy for sure."

"Our song will be way better," said DJ.

Grrr. Kate and Lucie growled.

Then Lucie whispered, "They are so obnoxious."

"With a capital *O*," said Kate.

"Check out those dogs," said DJ. "I wonder who they belong to."

"They're pretty cool-looking," said Danny.

"Omigosh," whispered Lucie. "They think we're cool!"

"Well, we are," said Kate.

Boing! Kate's tail went up again.

Shimmy, shimmy, shimmy. Lucie's backside wagged and wagged.

"Maybe we should take them home," said Danny.

Aaahhh! Kate's tail dropped, and Lucie stopped wagging.

"We've got to get out of here," whispered Lucie.

The dogs ran to the corner. But the light was red.

They heard DJ say, "I want the shaggy one."

"I want the white spotted one," said Danny.

"Ugh! Did you hear that?" said Lucie.

"Quick! In here," said Kate.

They raced down an alley and hid behind a Dumpster.

Sniff, sniff.

"This smells even better than the garbage can," said Lucie.

"Forget that! We've got to change back before Danny and DJ find us," said Kate.

"You're right. Let's do it," said Lucie.

"Do what?" said Kate.

Kate and Lucie looked at each other.

"What did we do to become dogs?" said Lucie.

Kate tried to remember. "First, we put on the necklaces," she said.

"Okay, then what?" said Lucie.

"We said something," said Kate.

"What did we say? Hurry! They're coming," said Lucie.

They heard Danny's and DJ's footsteps loud and clear.

"Think, Kate, what did we say?" said Lucie.

"Abracadabra?" said Kate.

"That doesn't sound right," said Lucie.

The boys were getting closer.

"Maybe they're behind that Dumpster," said DJ.

Lucie and Kate got so scared they barked. *Woof!*

"I hear them!" said Danny.

"That's what we did. We barked!" whispered Lucie. "Then what?"

"Um, um . . . we gave high fives," said Kate. "Quick! Let's do it."

First they woofed. Then they tapped their paws together. Nothing happened.

"We're still dogs," whispered Lucie.

"I know!" said Kate. "We have to woof and tap at the same time."

Together, they said *"Woofa-woof!"* and tapped their paws.

Woofa-wow! Their dog-bone necklaces lit up. With a pop and a whoosh, they were back to being girls. And not a second too soon. Danny and DJ were standing right in front of them.

"Hey, did you see a couple of dogs around here?" said DJ.

"Dogs? What dogs?" said Kate.

"One was shaggy, and one was white with spots," said Danny.

"You must be seeing things," said Lucie.

"Yes," said Kate. "In fact, you should go to your eye doctor."

"There were definitely two dogs here," said Danny.

"We don't know what you're talking about," said Lucie, looking innocent.

"Come on, Lucie," said Kate. "We have places to go."

"And things to do," said Lucie.

The girls linked arms and walked off with their dog-bone necklaces twinkling in the sun.

How Was Your Morning?

"Do you realize what just happened to us?" said Kate.

"You mean turning into dogs?" said Lucie.

"That would be it," said Kate.

"I wonder where the necklaces came from," said Lucie.

"They must have belonged to a magician," said Kate. "And now they belong to us!"

"This is so cool!" said Lucie.

"We can't have dogs. But now we can *be* dogs," said Kate.

When they got to their street, Kate said, "Want to come to my house for lunch?"

"Sounds good," said Lucie. "All I had since breakfast was that little pizza crust."

"Yuck. Don't remind me," said Kate.

Sniff, sniff. Lucie leaned over and started sniffing around Kate.

"Stop that! We're not dogs anymore," Kate said.

"I know that. I just want to make sure we don't smell doggy before we see your mom," said Lucie.

"You're right," said Kate. "Is there anything else? Do we have any dog hair on us?"

They checked themselves out and didn't find any clues that they had been dogs.

"Wait! Our necklaces!" said Kate.

"What about them? They won't give us away," said Lucie.

"I just realized we didn't pay for them," Kate said.

"We can go back later. Mrs. Bingly will understand," said Lucie.

When they got to Kate's house, her mom was on the phone.

"I'll bet she's talking to your mom," said Kate.

"Of course she is," said Lucie.

Their moms were best friends just like they were.

Mrs. Farber's job was baking cookies, cakes, and pies that were sold at the farmers market and at Didi's Bakery.

Mrs. Lopez was a teacher at the Little Apple School House.

They were single parents and helped each other out a lot.

"The girls just walked in," said Mrs. Farber.

"I'll put us all on speaker phone."

"Hi, Moms!" said Lucie and Kate together.

"I'm going to stay for lunch, okay, Mom?" said Lucie.

"Sure," said Mrs. Lopez. "Be sure to help clean up."

"I will," said Lucie.

"Bye, Christy," said Mrs. Lopez to Kate's mom.

"Later, Liz," Mrs. Farber answered.

After they hung up, Mrs. Farber took four blueberry pies out of one oven and four apple pies out of the other. She was going to deliver them to the bakery later that afternoon.

"How was your morning?" she asked the girls. "What did you do?"

Lucie and Kate looked at each other. They were glad Mrs. Farber was busy slicing cheese for their sandwiches. That way, she couldn't see the panic on their faces.

"What do we say?" mouthed Lucie. "That we barked and wagged and hid behind a Dumpster?"

"Don't be ridiculous," Kate mouthed back. "I'll handle this."

"We went to the thrift shop," she said. "We got these necklaces."

Kate's mom turned and looked. "They're cute," she said.

"We got them in time for Adopt-a-Dog Week," said Kate. "We're going to enter the Amos-on-the-Airwaves song-writing contest."

"We want to help dogs find homes," said Lucie.

"You two are good helpers," said Mrs. Farber. "And the way you love to rhyme, I bet you'll come up with something great."

She set down two glasses of cold milk. Then she gave each girl a plate with a gooey grilled cheese sandwich, cut into four triangles.

"Thanks, Mom," said Kate, arranging the triangles neatly on her plate.

"Thanks, Mrs. Farber. This looks delicious," said Lucie.

Out of the corner of her eye, Kate saw Lucie's head diving down to her plate. Kate poked her in the ribs.

"Stop that!" she whispered. "You're not a dog anymore."

"Just kidding," Lucie whispered back. She picked up the sandwich with her hand.

They ate their lunches, helped with clean-up, then disappeared into Kate's room. Kate closed the door behind them.

"I miss being dogs," said Lucie. She went down on all fours and wagged her behind.

"Me, too!" said Kate. "It was fun."

"Let's do it," said Lucie, waving her make-believe paws in the air.

"Okay," said Kate. "Ready . . . set . . ."

Woofa-woof! They barked and gave each other high fives.

Woofa-wow! Their dog-bone necklaces lit up. With a pop and a whoosh, they were dogs again!

"Uh-oh, I have a sudden urge to chew," said Lucie.

"Don't you dare look at my new slippers," said Kate.

"A dog's gotta do what a dog's gotta do!" said Lucie, leaping on one of the fluffy slippers.

Kate let out a bark.

"Girls, what is going on in there?" called Mrs. Farber.

"We're writing our dog song!" called Kate.

"We're putting in a woof or two!" said Lucie.

They woofed a couple more times.

"Let's go to the park," said Kate. "The dog park!"

"How do we get out without your mom seeing us?" said Lucie.

"This way," said Kate, heading for the open window.

The two dogs jumped out. They ran down the street, woofing all the way, with the pink dog bones on their collars twinkling in the sun.

Run, Dogs, Run!

As soon as they got to the park, they headed for the dog run. Inside, dogs were running around having fun while their owners chatted and sipped coffee.

Kate and Lucie were wondering how to get in when a man with a little dog opened the gate. He didn't notice Kate and Lucie as they slipped inside.

Once they were in, a group of dogs raced over and started sniffing them.

"This is a little scary," said Kate softly.

"What are you worried about?" said Lucie. "They're friendly."

"How do you know?" said Kate.

"Just watch. I'll tell them to sit," said Lucie. "My dog books say it's good to be the leader."

"Okay, tell them," said Kate.

"Dogs, sit!" said Lucie.

The dogs didn't know where the voice was coming from. They cocked their heads. They looked all around. Then they all sat.

Seeing them listen made Kate feel braver.

"Dogs, stay!" she said.

While Lucie and Kate trotted off, the dogs stayed where they were.

"See?" said Lucie. "We're the leaders!"

A ball came flying through the air.

"I'll get it!" called Lucie.

"Yuck, it's slobbery," said Kate.

"Who cares? We're dogs!" said Lucie.

She leaped up and grabbed the ball from

the air. Just then another ball came their way. Lucie leaped up and grabbed that one too. Now she had two balls in her mouth.

"Only you could do that," said Kate. "Do not try to get three!"

By then, the other dogs had started running around again. A huge dog came bounding toward them. Lucie dropped both balls.

"I'm not arguing with him," she said. "He looks like the leader to me."

"Good thinking," said Kate.

Suddenly, Kate's eyes opened wide.

"What's the matter?" said Lucie.

Kate stared hard at the spot behind Lucie.

"Woof-woof-woof!" Kate barked.

"What-what-what?" Lucie answered. She turned slowly, following Kate's eyes.

Standing right behind Lucie was the huge dog's owner, with her mouth hanging open in surprise.

"YIKES!" the dog's owner called over her shoulder.

A couple more people came over.

"What's going on?" said one man.

"These dogs are talking like people!" said the woman.

Uh-oh, thought Lucie.

We're in big trouble, thought Kate.

The man turned to the woman, looking puzzled.

"What are you saying?" he asked.

"I heard that shaggy dog talking. That dog said 'What's the matter' and 'What-what-what,'" said the big dog's owner.

"I know what-what-what's the matter," said the man. "You've been standing in the sun too long."

"No, I mean it," said the woman.

"Okay, let's see," said the man. He turned to Kate and said, "Speak!"

For a second, Kate froze. To a girl, "speak" means using words. But to a dog, "speak" means . . .

"Woof!" she barked.

Lucie barked, too. "Ruff!"

Other dogs joined in. Soon all the dogs in the run were barking their heads off.

"Look what you started," said another dog owner. He called to his bulldog, "Oliver, quiet!"

Another person called, "Fluffy, come!"

Soon all the people were calling their dogs, trying to get them to be quiet.

Kate and Lucie took the opportunity to walk off and get a drink from the water bowl.

"Phew! That was close," whispered Lucie.

"We have to be more careful from now on," said Kate.

As they started slurping up water, a scruffy

dog appeared. The dog sat down and started scratching. And scratching. And scratching!

"Uh-oh, maybe he has fleas," said Kate.

"If we catch fleas, our moms will be *so* mad," said Lucie.

"Run!" said Kate.

They raced out of the dog run as soon as the gate opened.

Kate and Lucie
to the Rescue

niff, sniff.

Kate's and Lucie's cold, wet noses went up in the air.

"Do you smell what I smell?" asked Lucie.

"You mean Banana-Fandana gum?" said Kate.

"Exactly," said Lucie.

"Do you hear what I hear?" said Kate.

Thunk, thunk, thunk.

"You mean Danny's basketball?" said Lucie.

"Yes! We'd better get away, or those boys will try to adopt us again!" said Kate.

They started running, but Danny and DJ had already seen them.

"It's those same dogs!" called DJ.

"You get in front. I'll get behind," said Danny.

"We'll close in on them," said DJ.

"Oh, no you won't!" whispered Kate.

"We're going to outsmart you," whispered Lucie.

Lucie ran left. Kate ran right. They zoomed around and got in front of DJ. Then they sped out of the park, leaving the boys far behind.

"That was close!" said Lucie. "One more minute and I would have belonged to DJ."

"And I would have belonged to Danny," said Kate.

"It's too terrible to talk about!" said Lucie.

Now that they were out of danger, they slowed down.

"Do you see what I see?" said Lucie, staring down the street.

Kate saw a dog sniffing around a garbage can. He was so skinny, his ribs were showing.

"He doesn't have a leash," said Kate.

"He doesn't even have a collar," said Lucie.

The dog was brown with four white paws and white at the tip of his tail.

"I once read that white on the tail means good luck," said Lucie. "But this dog doesn't look very lucky at all."

"Maybe his luck is changing," said Kate. "Let's turn back into girls and help. We can take him to the shelter."

"Girls can't just go up to a stray dog," said Lucie. "My dog books say it's dangerous."

"Okay, we'll stay dogs and get him to follow us," said Kate.

"Good idea," said Lucie.

Kate and Lucie turned and headed toward the animal shelter. They wagged their tails as if to say, "Come follow!"

They went a little way and peeked back to see if the dog was there. He was!

They kept going. They looked back again to make sure he was still there. He was, and now another dog was behind him.

"There's another unlucky dog," said Lucie.

The new dog had sad eyes and scraggly gray fur. She was limping and couldn't go very fast.

"Poor dog," said Lucie.

"We better slow down," said Kate.

They slowed down, and the dog was able to keep up.

"Looks like her luck is changing, too," said Lucie.

They kept going.

Yip! Yip! Tiny barks were coming from an alley. Two soft brown eyes peeked out from the corner of a building. A little tan dog looked like he wanted to join the line, but was too scared. He'd take a step out, then step back. Out and back.

"Come on, little dog," Kate said in a gentle voice.

He took a step out. Then another. And another. With a few more steps, the little tan dog was at the end of the line.

"Wow!" said Kate.

"Now we've got three dogs for the shelter."

"I hope they can find homes for them fast," said Lucie.

"They will," said Kate. "It's a good thing it's Adopt-a-Dog Week."

Just as they reached the shelter, the door opened. Maybe it really was going to be a lucky day for these dogs.

At the Shelter

Kate and Lucie led the three dogs inside. Behind the counter, a man was reading some papers. A woman was working at her computer.

The little tan dog yipped.

The woman stopped typing and looked up.

"Um, George," she said to the man, "there are five dogs standing by themselves in the lobby."

George put down his papers.

"One . . . two . . . three . . . four . . . five.

Yup, Carmen, there are five," he said. "How did they get in?"

"I have no idea, but let's go easy. We don't want to scare them," said Carmen.

George reached into the treat box, then stepped out from behind the counter. The three hungry strays came toward him.

"We'll need five leashes," said Carmen.

"We've got to get out of here," whispered Kate.

"Yeah, or we'll end up shelter dogs, too," Lucie whispered back.

While Carmen and George were looking at the gray dog's hurt paw, Kate and Lucie started walking backward. Slowly. Very slowly.

They turned toward the front door. Slowly. Very slowly.

But the door was shut tight.

"Uh-oh," whispered Lucie.

"Follow me!" whispered Kate.

She took off down the hall. Lucie took off after her. Running through the hallway wasn't so easy. Their paws went sliding across the slippery floor.

Kate slid into a wall. Lucie slid into a desk. They scrambled to get their paws back under them.

Workers saw Lucie and Kate running through the shelter. They came out to try to catch them. These workers had treats, too.

Kate and Lucie weren't looking for treats. They were looking for a place to hide.

"Quick! This way," said Lucie.

But they saw a wall ahead.

"Quick! That way," said Kate.

But more people were coming.

"Around this corner!" said Lucie.

There was a staircase. They ran down and heard the workers coming after them.

Kate and Lucie ran into an empty office. As fast as they could, they said "*woofa-woof*" and gave each other high paws. When they popped out of the office again, they were girls.

"Did you see two dogs?" asked one of the workers.

Kate stopped to catch her breath, then said, "Sure, there are lots of dogs."

"This is a shelter, isn't it?" said Lucie innocently.

"We mean two runaway dogs," said another worker.

"Runaways? Nope, didn't see any," said Kate, walking calmly toward the stairway.

"'Bye," said Lucie, waving over her shoulder.

Upstairs, Carmen and George passed by with the three strays on leashes.

"These dogs are so cute," said Carmen.

"I'm sure we'll find homes for them soon," said George.

Kate and Lucie walked toward the lobby with big grins on their faces.

"Hey, look at these," said Kate, pointing to two posters on the wall.

One poster said DO ADOPT IF . . .

The other said DON'T ADOPT IF . . .

Under each title was a list. The lists told you if you would or wouldn't be a good person to have a dog.

"Those posters just gave me an idea for the song," said Lucie.

"Is it a prizewinning idea?" said Kate.

"Could be," said Lucie.

"Okay, let's hear it," said Kate as they left the shelter.

A Song Is Born

Lucie started to sing:

> *Doo-wop, doo-wop!*
> *Do we adopt-adopt?*
> *Doo-wop, doo-wop!*
> *Do we not-adopt?*

"That's really good," said Kate. "Keep going."

"That's all I have," said Lucie. "I'm stumped."

Suddenly, they heard a boy's voice singing:

Tell me, can you be at home?

Can you buy me a bone?

The girls couldn't believe it! The voice belonged to DJ. The girls glared at him.

"Excuse me! This is *our* song," said Kate.

"We don't need help from any goofy boys," said Lucie.

"What's the matter? Those were good lines," said Danny.

Kate and Lucie thought about it. They didn't like to admit it, but Danny was right.

"Hey, what were you two doing in the shelter?" said Danny.

"Um, we were just doing some research," said Kate.

"That's right, for the song contest," said Lucie.

"What are you doing here?" asked Kate. "I hope you weren't thinking of adopting dogs."

"Nah. We were just passing by," said Danny.

"But now that you mention it, maybe we should get a couple of puppies," said DJ.

"Sounds good to me," said Danny. "I want a shaggy one. Like that one we saw on the street."

"And I'll get a spotted one," said DJ.

Kate and Lucie looked at each other.

"You saw dogs on the street?" said Kate.

"I bet they ran away from you," said Lucie. "Any sensible dogs would."

"The people at the shelter would never give innocent puppies to boys like you," said Kate.

"Dogs need proper homes with responsible owners," said Lucie.

"Owners who do not chew gum that will get stuck in their fur," said Kate.

"Owners who will not give them a headache bouncing a basketball," said Lucie.

"Do you think they're talking about us?" said DJ, snapping his gum.

"Could be," said Danny, bouncing his basketball.

"We've got to go now. We have a song to write," said Kate, marching off.

When they had gone a little way, Lucie got another idea and sang it.

Can you get to the vet
With your very own pet?

Danny and DJ sneaked up behind them. Danny made up a new line. Then DJ. Then Kate got an idea. They took turns singing back and forth. Before they knew it, they had a whole song.

"I guess we're all going to have to enter the contest together," said DJ.

"No way!" said Kate and Lucie.

"Way!" said DJ and Danny.

"Well, we did write it together," said Lucie.

"So we have to send it together," said Danny.

"Oh, okay," said Kate. "Lucie and I will send it to Amos."

"Don't forget to put our names on it," said Danny.

"In really big letters," said DJ.

The boys turned and walked off in one direction. The girls went off in the other.

It really was a pretty good song. The girls would write it up and mail it in as soon as they could.

Give Those Dogs a Bone

On the way home, the girls passed the Lucky Find Thrift Shop.

"Let's go in and pay for our necklaces," said Kate.

"Good idea," said Lucie, leading the way inside.

"Hi, Mrs. Bingly!" Kate and Lucie called when they went into the store.

"Hi, girls," said Mrs. Bingly.

"We owe you some money for the necklaces," said Kate.

"We forgot to pay for them this morning," said Lucie.

"Oh, that was when those dogs got in here," Mrs. Bingly said.

"Dogs? What dogs?" said Kate, poking Lucie in the ribs.

"Two dogs suddenly appeared, and I had to chase them away," said Mrs. Bingly.

The girls kept quiet and quickly counted out their money.

"Ooh, do you see what I see?" said Kate when they were finished.

"You mean that basket of Chewies Dog Bones?" said Lucie.

"That would be it," said Kate.

The idea of being dogs and chomping on those bones was very appealing. In fact, just

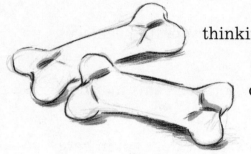

thinking about the bones almost made them drool on the counter.

"Let's each get one," said Kate. "After all, it's for charity."

"You mean it's for chewing!" said Lucie.

"Very funny," said Kate, handing the bones to Mrs. Bingly.

"We'll pay for these, too," Lucie said.

"Oh, have you gotten dogs, girls?" said Mrs. Bingly.

"Um, no, but it's Adopt-a-Dog Week," said Kate. "We might find a dog or two who'd enjoy them."

"That's very kind of you," said Mrs. Bingly.

The girls paid and went outside. Then they ran straight to the Dumpster.

Ready . . . set . . . woof! They barked and gave high fives.

Woofa-wow! Changing into dogs was easy now.

They started chomping on their bones. They really *had* found two dogs who enjoyed them.

"Let's take our bones home and bury them," said Kate.

"Great idea," said Lucie.

They ran all the way home to the garden their moms had made.

They jumped over the fence. Their dog noses were in overdrive.

"Do you smell what I smell?" said Kate.

"Could you mean carrots?" said Lucie.

"Exactly," said Kate. "Nice and crunchy."

They dropped their bones, dug up three carrots each, and chomped them down.

Then they found the lettuce patch.

"Tearing up lettuce is as much fun as chomping carrots," said Lucie.

"You're right. Let's do it!" said Kate.

They each tore up a few heads of lettuce. Then they grabbed their bones.

"Let's bury them here," said Kate, digging in.

"No. Here!" said Lucie, digging beside her.

"Wait, this is a good spot," said Kate, starting a new hole.

Marigolds and petunias went flying as the dogs dug holes all around the garden.

Finally, they each found just the right spot and buried their bones.

When they looked up, Kate said, "Do you see who I see?"

"You mean our mothers at the windows?" said Lucie.

"Exactly," said Kate.

"Do you hear what I hear?" said Lucie.

"Do you mean our mothers yelling?" said Kate.

"That would be it," said Lucie.

Their mothers came running outside.

"Scoot!" said Mrs. Lopez.

"Scat!" said Mrs. Farber.

"Scram, dogs, scram!" they said together.

"I think they're talking to us," whispered Kate.

"I think you're right," answered Lucie.

"Ready ... set ... scram!" they said together.

The dogs jumped over the fence, raced around the corner, and hid behind a mailbox. When they came out, they were girls again.

Kate and Lucie strolled back home.

They were just in time to hear Kate's mother saying, "I can't believe what those dogs did."

Lucie's mom said, "It's going to take forever to clean up the mess."

"Hi, Moms," said Kate and Lucie.

"Look what happened to our garden," said Lucie's mom.

"Two dogs got into it," said Mrs. Farber.

"What bad dogs!" said Kate.

"Shame on them," said Lucie.

Kate and Lucie were trying not to laugh. At the same time they were sorry. They really *had* been bad dogs.

"Go inside, Mom," said Lucie.

"You, too, Mom," said Kate. "We'll clean up."

"Really?" said Kate's mom.

"Absolutely," said the girls.

Lucie picked up a rake. Kate got a shovel.

They heard their moms talking as they walked away.

"Our girls sure are growing up," said Mrs. Farber. "It's wonderful how they jumped right in to help."

"They're really changing," said Mrs. Lopez.

"We sure are," said Kate, replanting a marigold.

"If they only knew," said Lucie, raking up the scattered lettuce.

And the Winner Is . . .

Arfa-arf! A few mornings later, Lucie's phone rang. Of course it was Kate.

"Want to go to the Sugar Shack?" she asked.

"I'm sleeping," said Lucie.

"I said Sugar Shack," said Kate.

"*Mmmff,*" mumbled Lucie.

"As in pink gumdrops," said Kate.

Lucie's eyes popped open. "Meet you in five!" she said.

When the girls got to the candy store, DJ and Danny were there.

"Did you mail in our song?" said DJ.

Kate and Lucie looked at each other.

"Oops!" Lucie said to Kate. "Did you mail it?"

"No. I thought you did," said Kate.

"No, you were going to," said Lucie.

The boys gasped. Kate and Lucie laughed.

"Gotcha!" said Lucie. "We were just kidding."

"We mailed it together," said Kate.

"Hi, girls!" called Izzy, the store owner. "I'll be right with you. I've got to go to the stockroom for more Banana-Fandana gum."

"I wonder who the gum could be for," said Kate.

"It couldn't possibly be for DJ, could it?" said Lucie.

"Very funny," said DJ.

Just then, the voice of Amos-on-the-Airwaves boomed out from Izzy's radio.

"Good morning, listeners! We have our contest winner! Make that winners!"

Wonka-wonk! Amos honked his horn.

"Who won? What are the names?" said Kate, hopping from one foot to the other.

Wonka-wonk! Amos honked again.

"The suspense is killing me," said DJ, snapping his gum.

"Come on, come on!" said Danny.

"And the winners are Lucie Lopez, Kate Farber, and—ah-ah-choo!" Amos sneezed.

DJ and Danny glared at Kate and Lucie.

"Did you leave our names off?" said Danny.

Honk! Amos blew his nose, then continued.

". . . DJ Jackson and Danny DeMarco!" he said.

"Yippee!"

"Yeowee!"

"Hooray!"

"Ya-hoo!"

Izzy came running out from the stockroom. When he saw the kids jumping up and down, he started jumping up and down, too.

"Why are we jumping?" Izzy asked.

"We won the Adopt-a-Dog song contest!" said Danny.

Amos's voice was still booming from the radio. "Are you listening in, prizewinners?" he said. "Come down to the studio this Saturday at 9 a.m. Be on time and be ready to sing your song!"

"Wow! We're gonna be on the radio," said DJ.

"Congratulations!" said Izzy, picking up a box of candies. "Have a caramel."

They all popped caramels into their mouths. Even Izzy.

They all started talking at the same time. It wasn't easy with caramel stuck to the roofs of their mouths.

"I'll lishen to oo on Shadaday," said Izzy.

"Thwank oo," said the kids as they headed to the door.

They waved good-bye to Izzy and raced home to share their prizewinning news.

Where's That Dog?

S aturday came around fast. Kate was so excited she was up at the crack of dawn. It was way too early to go to the radio station. But she was too excited to stay in bed.

Kate got dressed and dialed Lucie's number.

Arfa-arf! Lucie heard her phone ringing. She thought she must be dreaming.

Arfa-arf! She looked at her clock. It was 6:05 in the morning. Lucie wished she was dreaming.

Lucie picked up the phone. "Why are you calling so early?" she said in a sleepy voice.

"Let's go for a run! A dog run," said Kate.

"You're totally kidding, right?" said Lucie.

"Totally not. Totally serious," said Kate.

"Totally tired," said Lucie. "I'll call you later."

"Wait. Think about it. Sniffing lamp posts," said Kate.

"I'm hanging up," said Lucie.

"Chomping sticks," said Kate.

"I'm not kidding," said Lucie.

"Finding tasty scraps," said Kate.

That got Lucie's attention. "Okay! Meet you outside," she said.

As soon as they got to the park, Kate and Lucie changed into dogs.

They sniffed lamp posts. They chomped sticks.

Then Lucie sniffed out a tasty scrap under a bush.

"Wait right here," she said, diving in to get it.

Kate was waiting when suddenly a squirrel came running down the trunk of a tree. *Boing!* Kate's tail shot up in the air.

Kate loved a good squirrel chase. The squirrel ran down the path. So did Kate.

The squirrel crisscrossed back and forth. So did Kate. Kate was fast. But the squirrel was faster.

The squirrel disappeared over a hill. So did Kate.

Lucie came out from under the bush. Kate was nowhere to be seen.

"Where's that dog?" Lucie wondered.

She went off to find her. She trotted around the park, then wandered out. As she was leaving, Kate was coming back to the spot where she'd left Lucie.

"Where's that dog?" Kate wondered.

She looked around, but didn't see her.

"A-woo-woo!" she howled.

No answer.

"A-woo-woo-woo!" she howled again.

Still no answer.

This is terrible, thought Kate. *We've got to change back to girls and get to the radio station. But we can't change back unless we're together.*

"A-woo-woo-woo!" Kate howled one more time.

Lucie was too far away to hear Kate's howls. But she did hear a dog barking.

Behind a white picket fence, a tall Doberman pinscher was wagging his tail, looking her way. The Doberman looked like he wanted to play.

Shimmy, shimmy, shimmy! Lucie wagged her whole backside.

The Doberman ran and got a red rubber chicken toy. *Squeak! Squawk!* He tossed it up in the air. *Squeak! Squawk!* The radio station, the contest, and Kate floated right out of Lucie's head.

"I'll play with you!" Lucie called.

The toy dropped out of the Doberman's mouth. He cocked his head, looking puzzled.

"Oops!" said Lucie. "You're not used to dogs talking like people, are you?"

The Doberman slowly backed away.

"Don't go. Stay and play," said Lucie.

That did it! The Doberman turned and ran.

"Oh, well. I guess I should have woofed," Lucie said to herself. "If Kate was here, she'd be rolling her eyes at me."

Kate. The radio station. The contest. It all popped back into her head.

I've got to get to the park. I've got to find Kate! thought Lucie.

She ran down the street. An interesting smell from a tree came up on her right. She swerved to sniff it, then stopped herself.

I've got to find Kate, she thought.

She kept on running.

When she got close to the park, she heard, *"A-woo-woo-woo!"*

It was Kate!

"Ruff! Ruff!" Lucie called back.

She ran as fast as she could.

"A-woo-woo-woo!" she heard Kate howling again.

"Ruff! Ruff-ruff!" Lucie answered.

Kate and Lucie could hear each other. They could smell each other. But they couldn't see each other. That's because Kate was on one side of the park and Lucie was on the other. And there were trees in between.

"Ruff-ruff!"

"A-woo-woo!"

Kate and Lucie ran. They ran and ran. They didn't know it, but they were running in a circle around the same path, going in the same direction.

Lucie was near the water fountain. Kate was near the playground.

Then Kate was near the water fountain. Lucie was near the playground.

Suddenly, Kate got an idea. She turned around and started running the other way.

Lucie got the same idea at the same time. She turned around too.

They ran and ran. Just like before, they were going around the same path, in the same direction.

Lucie looked up at the clock.

"Only ten minutes to go! We've got to get to the station!" she said to herself.

Lucie was so horrified, she stopped right in the middle of the path. All of a sudden, a dog smashed into her.

"Kate!" said Lucie. "I've been looking everywhere for you!"

"I've been looking for you, too," said Kate. "Come on, let's go!"

As fast as they could, Kate and Lucie changed back into girls. They ran like the wind to the radio station.

Doo-Wop, Doo-Wop!

They made it to the radio station just in time. Danny and DJ were already there.

"Hi, girls," said Amos.

"How come you're panting so hard?" said DJ.

"It's a long story," said Kate.

"No time for stories," said Amos. "Are you ready to wow our listeners?"

"We're ready!" said the kids.

"I'll give you a hand signal when it's time to start," said Amos.

He set them in front of a line of micro-
phones.

"Testing! Testing!" said Danny, tapping the
mike.

"This is so cool," said DJ, way too loud.

Kate and Lucie rolled their eyes.

"You are so mature," said Kate.

"It's a good thing we're not on the air yet,"
said Lucie.

But they were about to be. Amos was
announcing them. He held up his hand and
gave the go-ahead, then the kids began to sing.

Doo-wop, doo-wop,
Do we adopt-adopt?

Doo-wop, doo-wop,
Or do we not-adopt?

Tell us, can you be at home?
Can you buy him a bone?

Will you brush her fur?
Go on walks with her?

Can you get to the vet
With your very own pet?

Will you wipe his drool?
Take him to dog-training school?

Then doo-wop, doo-wop,
Go adopt-adopt!

Doo-wop, doo-wop,
Your pet is waiting for yooooou!

As they sang the last note, the phones at the radio station started ringing like crazy.

People wanted to adopt dogs. They wanted to donate money to the shelter.

"Now, that's what I call a winning song!" Amos said over the airwaves. "Keep those calls coming in."

He played Elvis Presley singing "You ain't nothin' but a hound dog!" Then he turned to the kids. "And now for your prizes," he said. "First, you each get an Amos-on-the-Airwaves T-shirt. You can wear it while you listen to my show."

"Cool!" said Danny.

"Next, you all get tickets to the new movie *Dog Detectives*!" said Amos.

"Ooh, I want to see that," said Lucie.

"And now for the all-important prize number three," Amos continued.

He reached over to his desk and came back with a packet in his hand. "I am presenting each of you with an official Tuckertown Shelter badge. Wear it proudly. You will be

special volunteers helping the dogs at the shelter."

The kids loved their prizes. They thanked Amos and walked home together, singing:

Doo-wop, doo-wop!
Your pet is waiting for yooooou!

Here, Doggy-Doggies!

The next Saturday, the kids pinned on their badges and went to the shelter.

"Hi, Carmen! Hi, George!" Lucie called without thinking.

Kate poked her in the ribs. "We're not supposed to know their names," she hissed. "We were dogs the last time we were here."

"Oops," Lucie whispered back.

Luckily Carmen and George didn't notice.

"You wrote a great song, kids," said George.

"A lot of dogs have already been adopted thanks to you."

"Three of them are going to be picked up soon," said Carmen. "Their people are so excited. They've already named them."

"Want to help get the dogs ready?" said George.

"Sure!" the kids said together.

Carmen and George led them to a room down the hall. As soon as Kate and Lucie stepped inside, they saw three dogs in a pen. They were the same ones Kate and Lucie had brought to the shelter. The dogs started barking and jumping, trying to get near the girls.

"Wow," said Carmen. "Those dogs like you."

"It's almost as if they know you already," said George.

Lucie and Kate tried to keep a straight face. The dogs did know them already.

"If the dogs knew them, they'd be running the other way," Danny said to DJ.

"Very funny. Dogs love us," said Kate.

"They only run away from you two," said Lucie.

Carmen interrupted. "We want the dogs to look good for their new owners," she said. "Will you brush them and put ribbons on?"

"Ribbons?" said Lucie. "That's the job for me!"

The kids got brushes and a big box of ribbons.

"You brush, I'll tie," said Lucie.

Kate brushed the brown-and-white dog. Lucie tied on a light-blue ribbon.

DJ brushed the little tan dog. Lucie gave him a yellow ribbon.

The gray dog had a bandage around her

hurt paw. Danny brushed carefully around it, and Lucie tied a big red ribbon around the dog's neck.

Just as they were finishing, a family with two little girls came in. The little girls were so excited.

"Hi, doggy," they said to the brown-and-white dog. "We're going to call you Buddy."

Behind the family was a gray-haired woman. "Here's my sweet Muffin," she said, picking up the little tan dog. He licked her cheek, and she carried him out.

Now only the gray one was left. She looked sad. Then two young men came in.

"Gloria, you look terrific!" said one.

Her ears perked up.

"We'll take really good care of you," said the other.

The kids spent the next hour helping other dogs who were still waiting for homes. Then it was time to leave.

"Thanks for helping, kids," said Carmen.

"It was fun. We'll see you next week," said Kate.

Outside, they walked down the street, lined up four across. They started bouncing Danny's basketball one to another.

"That was so great," Kate said. "I love brushing dogs."

"My favorite is feeding them," said DJ.

"Did you see that little white one fall asleep in my lap?" said Lucie. "It was so sweet."

Danny turned to DJ. "Hey, I wonder what happened to those two dogs we saw the other day."

"You mean the spotted one and the shaggy one?" said DJ. "Yeah, they were really cool."

Kate and Lucie snorted, trying not to laugh.

Then they looked at each other, with a gleam in their eyes. They were about to have some fun.

The girls hung back and disappeared behind some bushes.

They whispered, "*Woofa-woof!*" and gave each other high fives. Their dog-bone necklaces lit up. There was a pop and a whoosh, and suddenly two dogs were running to catch up with the boys.

"Look! Those are the dogs!" said Danny.

"Here, doggy-doggies!" called DJ.

The dogs danced back and forth in front of the boys. Then they ran around the corner where they couldn't be seen and changed back. When the boys caught up, they saw the two girls.

"Looking for something?" said Lucie.

"Did you see those two dogs?" said DJ.

"Dogs? What dogs?" said Kate.

"You're seeing things again," said Lucie. She bent down to tie her shoe.

When the boys got ahead of them, the girls ducked behind a tree and came out barking.

The dogs ran in circles around the boys. Then they ran off to change again.

When they came back as girls, DJ said, "You had to see the dogs that time."

"We did! We saw their tails disappear right around that corner," said Kate, pointing.

"Come on!" said Danny. "Let's find them."

The boys took off running.

"Do you think they'll find those dogs?" said Kate.

"In their dreams," said Lucie.

"Those boys are so goofy," said Kate.

"But we did write a great song together," said Lucie. "And we had fun helping the shelter dogs with them."

"Speaking of dogs, I know two who could use a new toy," said Kate.

"I know just the dogs you're thinking of," said Lucie. "New squeaky balls would be very nice."

The two friends linked arms and headed for the pet store, with their dog-bone necklaces twinkling in the sun.

THE END

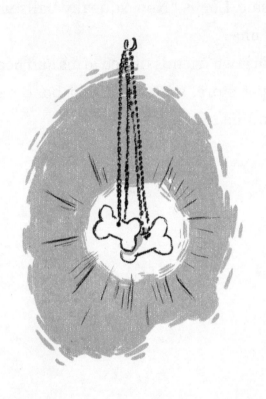

If you love dogs,
bark three times and
turn the page.

Woof-Ha-Ha! Dog Funnies

What kind of dog likes to take baths?

A shampoodle.

What time is it when ten German shepherds are running after two poodles?

Ten after two.

Why are Dalmatians not good at playing hide-and-seek?

They're always spotted.

Why is a dog so hot in summer?

Because he wears a fur coat and pants.

Knock-knock.

Who's there?

Orange.

Orange who?

Orange you going to take me for a walk?

Dog Heroes

English Bulldog Rescues Kittens

Six kittens were trapped inside a burlap bag in the middle of a deep lake. They were sinking fast and would have drowned if it hadn't been for an English bulldog named Napoleon.

Bulldogs are known for being poor swimmers, but that didn't stop Napoleon from doggy-paddling out, grabbing the bag, and pulling the kittens to shore.

Some people think dogs and cats are enemies, but Napoleon didn't agree. The kittens were saved and taken to an adoption center.

Beagle Phones for Help

Belle was a companion dog to a young man with a serious illness. When he became unconscious, Belle sprang into action.

She couldn't give her owner medical treatment, but she was trained to bite down on the number 9 of the cell phone to speed dial for help.

Rescue workers rushed to the scene and saved the man's life. They couldn't have done it without Belle, the heroic beagle.

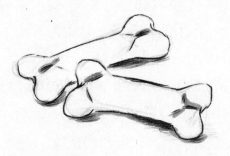

Mix-and-Match Dogs

There are hundreds of dog breeds—from the tiny Chihuahua to the huge Great Dane. Kate and Lucie are mixed breeds.

Here are some breeds.

Here are some mixes.

Can you guess which mixes came from which breeds? It's not always easy to tell!

Woofa-Wow!

What kind of mixed breed would you like
to be?

Find a friend and say:

Woofa-woof!

Pop . . . whoosh . . . wow!

Look at us—

We're dogs now!

A Dog of My Own

By Stephanie Calmenson

Sketch by Stephanie

Every year when I was a kid, my parents asked, "What would you like for your birthday?" Every year, I said, "Please, please, please can I have a dog?" Every year, they said, "No, we're not home enough to take care of one." So I was a dogless kid.

Years later, I finally got myself the birthday present I'd always wanted—a dog of my own. She was a black-and-white fur ball, and I named her Rosie, hoping she'd have a rosy disposition. She did!

She was also very funny. She'd bounce

down the street with her long hair over her eyes, then suddenly drop down and roll over, waiting for a passerby to give her a belly rub. That's how she got her nickname, Rollover Rosie.

Rosie was so sweet and funny, I wanted to share her with people who needed to be cheered up. So we became a volunteer team, visiting people in hospitals, nursing homes, and special schools. To share her with even more people, I wrote a book called *Rosie: A Visiting Dog's Story*.

Rosie lived a good, long life and is in dog heaven now. She made many people happy and is still cheering them up from the pages of her book. Good dog, Rosie! You were so worth waiting for.

My Life with Dogs

By Joanna Cole

Sketch by Joanna

Just like Stephanie, I spent my whole childhood longing for a dog, and just like Stephanie's family, mine said no, no, no. I got a goldfish, a turtle, a parakeet, and two cats. But no dog.

Maybe that's why when I grew up and had a home of my own, I got one dog after another until I eventually had five of them.

Two of my dogs were tiny—Taffy and Muffy. Taffy was taffy-colored, and Muffy was a little muffin. Three dogs were big—Harley, Suki, and Tater. Harley was named after a motorcycle. Suki came from a nursery rhyme.

And Tater got his name because he ate a whole bowl of raw potatoes when he was a puppy.

Fast-forward twenty years, and all my dogs are happy in dog heaven. Maybe they're running around with Stephanie's Rosie. Meanwhile, my grandchildren, Annabelle and William, got a teeny black Chiweenie named Gracie. (You might be asking, What is a Chiweenie? It's a cross between a Chihuahua and a dachshund.) Luckily for me, we live near each other, so even though Gracie lives at Annabelle and William's house, there's a dog in my life again.

GOFISH

Stephanie Calmenson

© Carlos Chiossone

What did you want to be when you grew up?
A kindergarten teacher.

When did you realize you wanted to be a writer?
In graduate school, while studying for my masters degree in education, I took a course called Writing for Children. The first story I wrote, "Buffy's Wink," was published in *Humpty Dumpty's Magazine for Little Children*.

What's your most embarrassing childhood memory?
Fortunately, I've forgotten.

What's your favorite childhood memory?
Walking my neighbors' dog near the beach on summer mornings. The family liked to sleep late, so they left their door open for me. I'd slip in to get Lucky, their schnauzer, and off we'd go.

As a young person, who did you look up to most?
My uncle Eli was quite tall, so I'd have to bend my head way back. . . .

What was your favorite memory of school?
Every Friday afternoon, my fourth grade teacher, Mrs. Riley, read aloud to us—everything from *Pippi Longstocking* to *Romeo and Juliet.*

What are your hobbies?
I'd say that writing is both my work and my hobby because I'd write even if I didn't get paid.

What was your first job?
In our late teens, my friend Karen and I ran a summer program for preschoolers and had so much fun. Our love of working with young children carried over into adulthood. Karen became a preschool teacher. I taught kindergarten, and most of the books I've written are for young children.

What sparked your imagination for *No Dogs Allowed*?
Joanna and I were trying to come up with an idea that would be fun to work on together. Since we're good friends who both love dogs, we wanted to put friendship and dogs in our story. One day we were talking about growing up as dogless kids, and then knew we had to write about kids like us—kids who want a dog more than anything but can't have one.

If you could be any dog, what kind would you be?
Any poodle mix. No, wait, a Lab. Hold on, a dachshund! Ooh, ooh—a basset hound! Hmm, maybe a Great Dane . . .

Did you ever pretend you were a dog when you were little?
I did! A shaggy mixed breed. (See below for shaggy.)

Do you have any dogs?
My first dog was Rosie, who was sweet and shaggy and became a Visiting Dog, cheering up people in hospitals, nursing homes, and special schools. I wrote about her in *Rosie, A Visiting Dog's Story*. My dog Harry, who's beside me as I write, is a long-haired, chocolate-dappled dachshund. He's the star of *May I Pet Your Dog?: The How-to Guide for KIDS Meeting DOGS (and DOGS Meeting KIDS)*. My dogs are great company and great inspiration.

What challenges do you face in the writing process, and how do you overcome them?
Sometimes I'll get an idea but am not sure how to turn it into a book. So I'll start writing, and if one approach doesn't work, I'll try another. And another. And another. If I'm still stuck, it's time to walk the dog.

Which of your characters is most like you?
Lucie and I have a lot in common. (Now how did that happen?!) Like Lucie, I couldn't have a real dog, but I had lots of stuffed

dogs. When I was Lucie's age, I had long bangs that hung down into my eyes. And, like Lucie, I love to read about dogs.

What makes you laugh out loud?
When my dog Harry smiles at my friend Carmen. It happens if she talks to him in a wacky voice. His top lip goes up, which makes his nose scrunch up, and it's the funniest thing in the world.

If you could live in any fictional world, what would it be?
I'd live in the Swiss Alps with Heidi, Grandfather, Peter, his grandmother, and the goats. Of course, I'd have a few dogs.

What was your favorite book when you were a kid?
You guessed it—*Heidi*.

Do you have a favorite book now?
Uh-oh, this is like deciding what kind of dog to be. Let's see—*David Copperfield*. No, wait, *Remains of the Day*. But I love *Light in August*. And *The Carrot Seed*. That's it, *The Carrot Seed*.

What is your favorite word?
Serendipity.

What's your idea of fun?
Walking a dog. My dog. My neighbor's dog. Any dog. I love to walk a dog.

If you could travel in time, where would you go and what would you do?
I'd go back to Rockaway summers, where I'd ride my bike, fly my kite, walk Lucky the schnauzer, float in the ocean, and make castles in the sand.

Do you ever get writer's block? What do you do to get back on track?
I don't worry about writing for *work*. I just write for *fun*—about anything from dogs to doughnuts. Of course, being a children's book writer, I often turn those ideas into books. So much for writer's block!

What do you wish you could do better?
Sing.

What would your readers be most surprised to learn about you?
Growing up, I was afraid to write and never in a million years thought I'd end up making my living as a writer.

What do you want readers to remember about your books?
The thing I'd like readers to remember about my books is they *enjoyed* reading them.

GO FISH

Joanna Cole

© Annabelle Helms

What did you want to be when you grew up?
I never had the slightest idea what I wanted to be. It was just pure luck that I ended up being a writer.

What was your favorite thing about school?
I loved science class, writing school reports, and reading science books from the library.

When did you realize you wanted to be a writer?
I had always loved to write, but I never imagined that an ordinary person like me could be a real writer. Then when I was a young adult, I got a job at a news magazine answering the letters to the editor. I saw a lot of people like me who were writing for a living, and I realized that I *could* be a writer.

I asked myself, What should I write? The answer came

easily. I would write what I had loved as a kid: science books for children. Later I branched out and wrote humorous story-books as well.

What sparked your imagination for *No Dogs Allowed*?
I always wanted a dog when I was a child, but my parents said, "No, no, no." I had a goldfish, a turtle, a parakeet, and two cats. But never a dog. So writing about girls who couldn't get a dog was natural for me.

How did you and Stephanie decide to write a series together?
Stephanie and I have been friends for a long time, and we've written books together. We often say to each other, "How about this idea?" "How about that idea?" When we thought of writing about girls who wanted dogs, we knew it was the right idea!

What's your favorite childhood memory?
Making a garden with my aunt and uncle.

What are your hobbies?
Reading and writing.

What was your first job, and what was your "worst" job?
I had a job washing out test tubes in a health department lab. I liked it quite well. Another time I worked the night shift on an

assembly line making TV sets. I was very bad at it. I couldn't work fast enough, and things were always piling up behind me and slowing everyone else down. One night the foreman came over and said, "Honey, this isn't really working out for you, is it?" Wow! Was I glad to hand in my tools and get out of there.

What book is on your nightstand now?
I've just finished a wonderful novel for middle graders, *Counting by 7s,* by Holly Goldberg Sloan.

Where do you write your books?
I once lived in a house that had a built-in desk facing a beautiful view of a brook running through the woods. People would come over and say, "Oh, this must be where you write!" No way! When I write, I don't look around. I look at the computer screen. So I write in the attic, which doesn't have a view at all.

Did you ever pretend you were a dog when you were little?
No, but I did pretend to be a horse. Actually, I pretended I was the horse and the rider at the same time. For a while, I took a piece of rope to school and hung it under my coat. At the end of the day, I would "ride" home using the rope as reins.

Do you have any dogs?
I have had five dogs in my life: Taffy, Muffy, Harley, Suki, and Tater. I also like guinea pigs as pets. Once I had eight of them at

the same time. Most recently I had two named Chuck and Wee Chuck. Sadly, they got very old and finally died. Now I have two new ones: Pepper and Paprika. They are adorable, of course.

Which of your characters is most like you?

There are two characters like me. First is Arnold in The Magic School Bus. That's because, like him, I am not adventurous; I like to stay home and do quiet things.

The other is Ms. Frizzle. I'm not wacky like her, but I do like to explain science. That's not surprising, since that's what I do most of the time in my writing.

What makes you laugh out loud?

My husband, Phil, says funny things all the time. It's one of the reasons I married him. Another is that he likes dogs.

What do you do on a rainy day?

Get out my umbrella!

What's your idea of fun?

Playing with my grandchildren. (But when I get tired and want to take a break, they do not think I am any fun at all.)

What is your favorite word?

Chocolate.

Who is your favorite fictional character?

Anne of Green Gables.

Do you ever get writer's block? What do you do to get back on track?

I often get scared to write, especially when I come to a point where I don't know exactly what to write next. Then I'll avoid going to my desk. It's awful.

However, a few years ago, a friend gave me a tip that works for me: instead of starting to write in the usual way, tell yourself that you will work just for ten minutes. After that, you *must* stop. The next day, work for fifteen minutes. And so on. After a while, you find yourself back in the swing of things.

What's the best advice you've ever had?

The ten-minute trick.

What do you wish you'd known when you were younger?

The ten-minute trick!

Kate and Lucie's adventures continue!

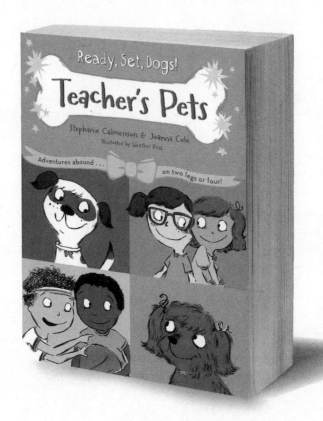

Turn the page for a sneak peek of
Teacher's Pets

Chompy Chips

Kate and Lucie let Danny and DJ get ahead of them. Then they ducked behind a hedge, where no one could see them.

The girls had discovered the magic of the necklaces by accident the day they found them at the Lucky Find Thrift Shop. Now they knew just what to do.

Kate and Lucie faced each other. At the exact same time, they said "Woofa-woof!" and gave each other high fives.

Woofa-wow! That did it! Their dog-bone

necklaces lit up. With a pop and a whoosh, Kate and Lucie weren't girls anymore. They were dogs!

No matter how many times it happened, they still couldn't believe it.

One dog was shaggy with ginger-colored fur that hung down almost to her eyes. The fur looked just like Lucie's bangs.

The other dog was white with tan spots, dark brown ears, and a brown patch around the eyes. The spots looked a lot like Kate's freckles. The dark brown ears were like her pigtails. And the patch around the eyes was like her glasses.

Instead of their necklaces, both dogs had silver collars with pink dog bones hanging down.

"We did it! We're dogs!" said Kate.

"It's show time!" said Lucie.

They trotted out from behind the hedge,

wagging their tails. They ran to catch up with Danny and DJ, then danced back and forth ahead of them.

The boys had seen them around the neighborhood before.

"Hey, there are those cool dogs again," said Danny. "Maybe we can get them to follow us to school," said DJ.

"Good idea," said Danny.

He turned to Kate and Lucie and said, "Dogs, follow!"

Instead of following, the dogs walked backward away from the boys.

"Wait! I know what to do!" said DJ.

He dug into his backpack and pulled out an open bag of Chompy Chips.

Boing! Kate's tail went up in the air. She loved Chompy Chips!

"Yoo-hoo, doggies!" DJ called, holding one out.

Shimmy-shimmy-shimmy! Lucie didn't wag just her tail. She wagged her whole behind. She loved Chompy Chips, too.

"Come and get it!" called Danny.

"Chompy Chips are so delicious," whispered Lucie. Kate came to her senses fast.

"They are not delicious enough to make us go with those obnoxious boys," she whispered. "Follow me."

The dogs raced ahead of the boys and ducked behind the post office.

Without wasting a second, they barked "Woofa-woof!" as they tapped their paws together. *Woofa-wow!* The dog bones on their collars lit up, and Kate and Lucie were back to being girls. "Do you think they'll give us any chips now?" said Kate.

"No way," said Lucie.

The boys came running. After they passed, the girls came back out and caught up with them.

"Did you see two dogs?" said DJ.

"Dogs? What dogs?" said Kate.

"I don't see any dogs," said Lucie.

They rolled their eyes at Danny and DJ.

"Are you sure you know what dogs look like?" said Kate.

"Four legs? Furry? Waggy tails?" said Lucie.

Danny looked disgusted.

"It's no use talking to these goofy girls," he said, turning into the school yard.

DJ followed, stuffing the bag of chips back into his pack.

"We knew we wouldn't get any Chompy Chips," Lucie whispered.

DJ and Danny ran over to talk to some of their friends.

"We'll let you know if we see those dogs!" Kate called after them.

The girls linked arms and walked into school with their dog-bone necklaces twinkling in the sun.